THE LITTLE ¢OPPER PENNY

Stephenie Barker

Illustrated by
Cynthia Meadows

BROWN BOOKS KIDS

This is a work of fiction. Any similarity to real persons, living or dead, is coincidental and not intended by the author.

The Little Copper Penny

Brown Books Kids
16250 Knoll Trail Drive, Suite 205
Dallas, Texas 75248
www.BrownBooksKids.com
(972) 381-0009

A New Era in Publishing®

ISBN 978-1-61254-943-9
LCCN 2016953357

Printed in the United States
10 9 8 7 6 5 4 3 2 1

For more information or to contact the author, please go to www.TheLittleCopperPenny.com.

Dedication

For Jason. Love, Stephenie.

Acknowledgments

Thank you to my family and friends for their encouragement and support. Also, a special thank you to Brown Books for believing in *The Little Copper Penny*. You made my dream come true!

"Grandpa Wheat, why do the other coins say we're worthless?" asked the Little Copper Penny. Grandpa Wheat was a wise old penny dated 1922. He had been around for a very long time, and the Little Copper Penny was sure that Grandpa knew everything.

Grandpa Wheat looked at the shiny new penny and said, "They are quite wrong about our worth, Little Copper Penny. Let me tell you a story I learned way back when I was new. I'm sure it will cheer you up."

A little-known fact about us coins

is pennies count the best.

But those silver coins, they disagree since

we're valued so much less.

The quarter states with confidence,

"Of math, you know the least.

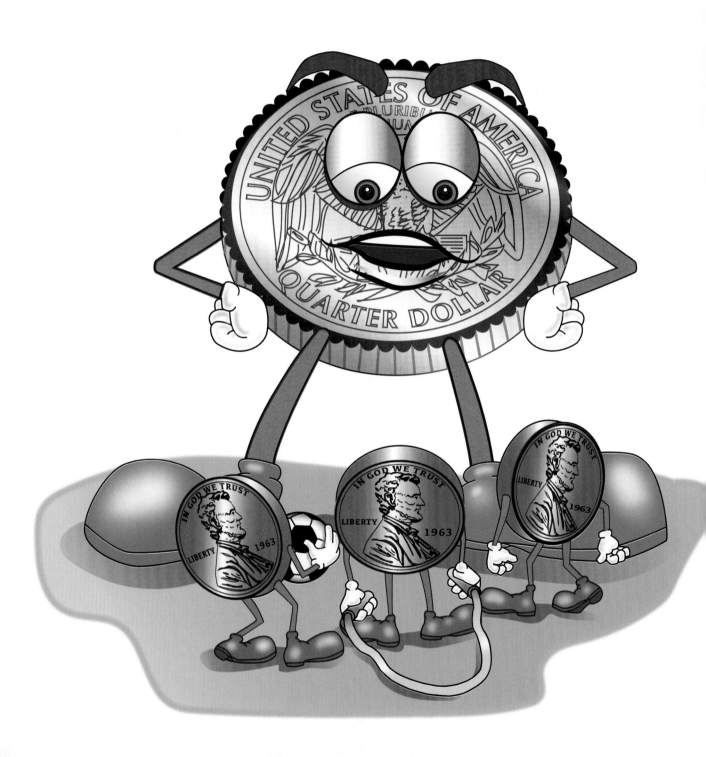

Of pennies,
you'd need twenty-five
to equal one of me.

And even then, with all your friends,

you pennies know the score.

What for you would take a hundred,

well, I can do with four."

And then the dime, in record time,

does add defiantly,

"The quarter has you there, my friend,

as anyone can see.

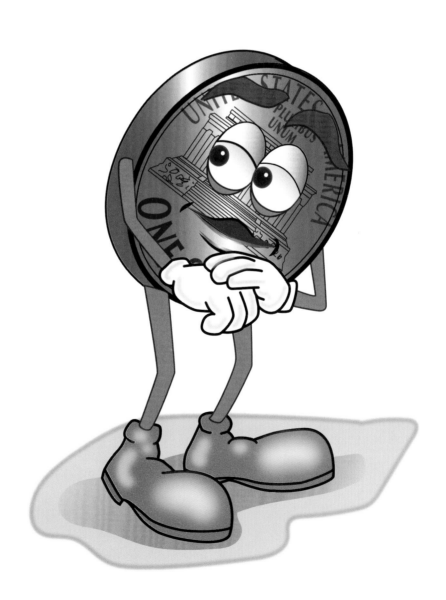

But if I may, it's not just worth.
A balance must be struck.
I'm ten of you but smaller still.
And that's more bang for the buck."

The nickel's proud and often loud—
of course he'd verbalize:
"The dime has put in his two cents.
Now, let me give you five.

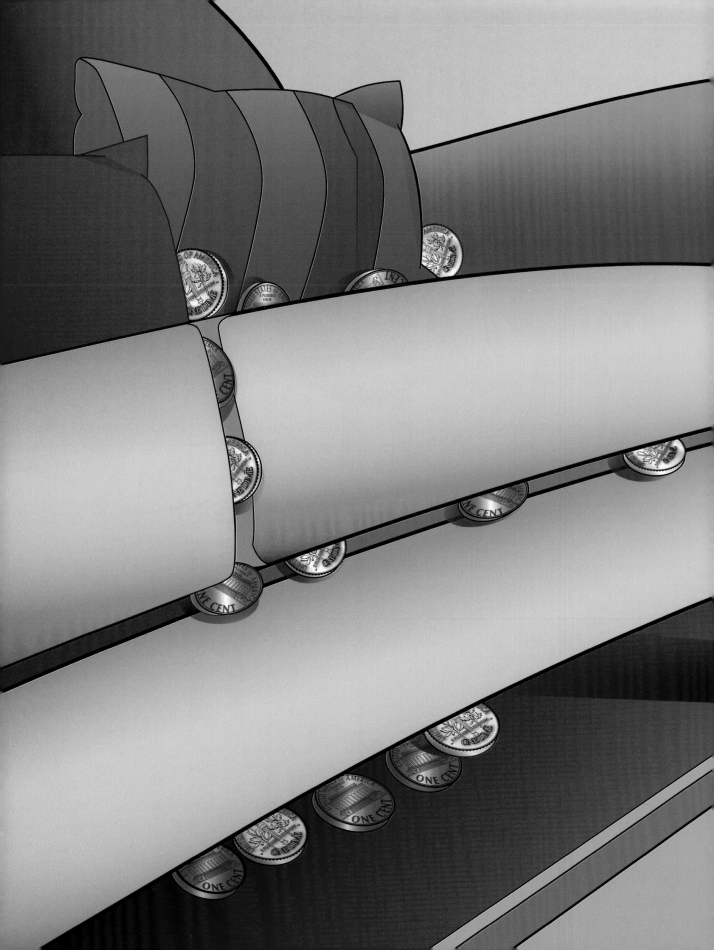

These smaller coins, they are
confused how size is relevant.
Pennies and dimes are often lost,
but the nickel's always spent."

They've made their point. It's understood
that as they all change hands,
they think their size and value
will score a high demand.

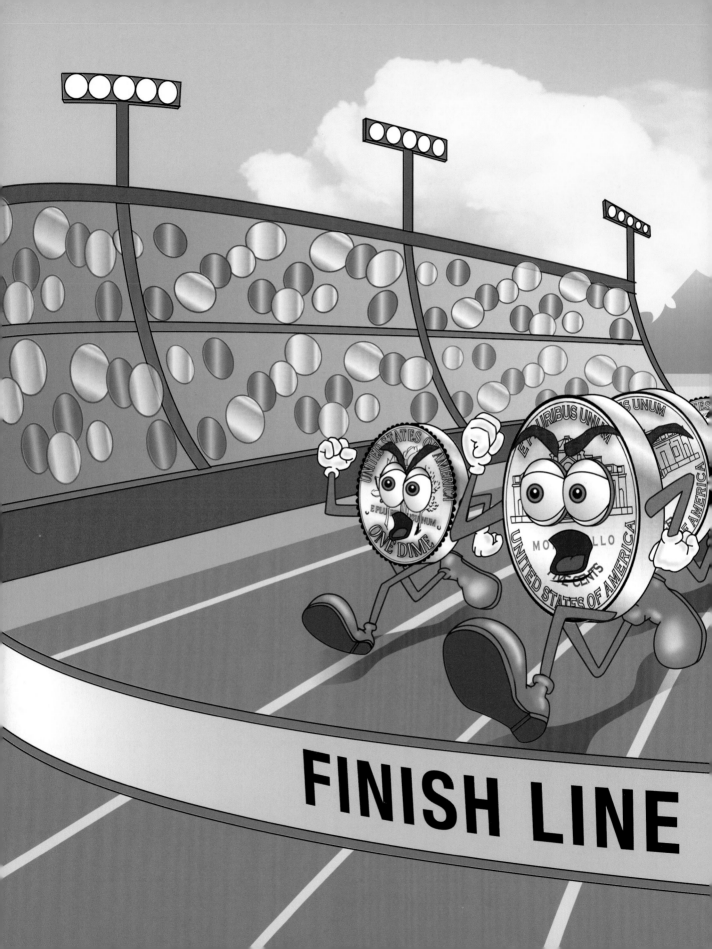

But what about the way they count?
They do it rapidly,
by fives and tens—round numbers, then,
are all they'll ever be.

But what about the threes and fours—
the numbers in between?
Don't ever ask a quarter
to count to sweet sixteen.

I've yet to see a single dime
that stopped itself at nine
or a big old shiny nickel
that noticed other primes.

But now, you see, my point is clear: The penny has its place.
You've simply got to have some cents to make the proper change.

"See, Little Copper Penny? We do have value. The counting starts with us and ends with us. Without us, you're either too short or always over," Grandpa Wheat explained. "The fact is there has to be enough of us to cover the rest. Just look around—you will find us everywhere. Collect us, and we add up quickly."

"Wow!" exclaimed the Little Copper Penny. "We pennies do have value! Grandpa Wheat, I'm glad I'm a penny."

About the Author

As a young couple, Stephenie Barker and her husband learned the importance of saving money and planning for the future, and the value of money became a key principle they wished to pass on to their children. Through her real estate career, Stephenie has had the privilege of helping other young buyers navigate the difficulties of savings and investment. Though her own children are grown, Stephenie hopes that *The Little Copper Penny* will communicate to children both the value of money in its least denominations and the value in themselves.

About the Illustrator

Cynthia Meadows, a native Texan, draws and paints on anything she can find. Whether it was cartoons on the sides of her homework in elementary school, paintings as Christmas gifts, murals or faux finishes on walls, or illustrations and storyboards for advertising agencies, she has continually decorated the world. Cynthia's desire to look inside characters is the reason she loves to illustrate children's books, to create characters, and to give the reader a positive, often humorous, view of life.